i

c

o

p

e

For more information, find CCM at:

http://copingmechanisms.net

TODAY I AM A BOOK

xTx

~ 1.
Today I Am A Dedication

Today I am a dedication.

Today, and everyday *you* are my driving force.

Thank you, Roxane Gay, for making me believe.

Still.

~ 2.
Today I Am A Surgeon

Today I am a surgeon. I am in my bathrobe. It is pink around the coffee stains and sags on me like a wet dishcloth. The cigarette burns pepper it like buckshot. One day it will become a screen door or mosquito netting. Surprisingly enough, the belt is still secured in its loops, although both ends of it are now gray-brown. It's an ugly color that doesn't need to exist. Nobody would miss it. God would even admit it's a mistake. The color spawned because I never tie it. I just let the ends dangle and they do whatever they want. Good thing I never had kids, I can't even parent a bathrobe.

Did you know that pink is the most popular color of ladies' bathrobes? I do. Look it up. I did careful research before I bought it. My mom deserved only the best. "Only the best for my dear mother!" That's exactly what I said after she opened it. After she gushed her thanks at me, holding it to her chest like a newly-birthed infant. "Oh, Michael!" she said, her voice bubbled with goo that she proceeded to hack up into the small towel she kept next to her cigarettes.

Oh, how she clutched it! Remember how I used to fit in her arms? Of course you don't. But she loved that bathrobe. Wore it every day until the end. That's when

I took it. Now it's my bathrobe.

I start most mornings sitting outside, smoking my breakfast, doing my own hacking. On better days I'll try to have a bowl of cereal. Try to eat food like normal people do. That never goes the way I want. It usually just sits there until I get angry and start throwing the little colored nuggets off my deck into my downstairs neighbor's barbeque grill. Rainbow hail.

My deck looks like a wrecked pirate ship; the faded green, rip-shredded sun umbrella, its battered flag. The wood is splintered and warped. Everything tilted. I'm surprised the whole of it hasn't fallen into my neighbor's yard. It's only a matter of time until it does and I hope I'm sitting on my deck when it happens. Anything to speed up this process.

My house is wedged in like pie—a slice between the Santa Monica Freeway on one side, and the Robertson Avenue off ramp on the other. It's a peninsula. When I am out on my deck, I face west and the eastbound traffic on either side of me blows my hair back. When I'm out on my deck and stoned, it feels like I am standing right there amongst the cars. The constant noise soothes me. I am a baby. I am something needing its mother.

I have my mother's hands. If my hands were severed from my wrists and found next to a dumpster in a grocery bag, the authorities would assume they belonged to a woman. The skin is baby smooth. The fingers, thin and long. The nails, almond-shaped and well-manicured. When I was young, my mother and I would play "nail salon" and she would paint our nails. She would always paint them the same color. Afterwards, she'd lift her finished work by the wrists and exclaim, "The hands of a surgeon!!!" Then we'd go looking for recyclables, making sure to bring our metal "grabbers" and rubber gloves so as to not mar our perfect manicures. It never mattered, they'd always get ruined.

"Fix me, baby," she'd say, slumped in her chair, waggling her fingers, eyes closed.

I'd go get the polish remover and some toilet paper and she'd fall asleep by the time I'd get to the third finger. Her brownest one.

I'd do mine after. My surgeon fingers not yet brown. Took only until 14 when that happened. We shared the same brand. Of course we did. We shared the same everything. Even now. Same disease wrapped in the same bathrobe. Except I have nobody here to "fix me, baby."

~ 3.
Today I Am A Black And Gray Tattoo Of A Skull With Snakes Coming Out Of Its Mouth

Today I am a black and gray tattoo of a skull with snakes coming out of its mouth.

Wherein sleeps the boy.

Wherein sleeps I.

Curled there, in the part of him that has yet to show itself.

We are tangled; me—this invisible, and he—never ready to come out. Until he does. With force.

In a world where mothers are hunched, thin-stemmed blossoms with cracked-closed mouths. In a world where fathers are men **are men** are all they believe themselves to be. In a world where there is one strong way and no tolerance for lesser, I become.

As does the boy.

Unaware, he often scratches the place where I will

eventually surface.

I can feel him wanting me.

Is there a burning?

His mother is a servant. His mother is a warm, wet place for his father to stick his dick.

Your mother is a hole. Call your mother a hole. That's it, boy. A hole.

His father laughs at his son who is seven who is calling his mother a hole. The son loves making his father laugh because it is an event that is serenity-rare.

His father.

Laughing.

On his account.

The hole makes them breakfast. The hole is allowed to eat their leftovers with cigarette ash garnish while the father watches and the boy is told to watch.

Put whatever you want in the hole. I do.

Whatever you want...

The mother is hole for a long time and whenever the boy forgets and cries "mommy," the father's fist reminds him, and soon, he never forgets and soon, he never has to be made to watch what the hole is made to eat/endure because pleasing his father is the only thing and the mother is only a hole that does whatever they tell it.

After I appear, he will create many like his mother hole because he learned from the best. A trail of two-legged, singular-cunted wreckage in a forgotten wake behind him, wherein swims the hole.

Wherein swims his father.

He is an incredible wrestler so his losses are rare. When they *do* occur there is an aftermath in which I take on more shape. With his victories comes only a simple beating, nothing like what his losses deliver.

It is a life where there is no surface, only ocean. There is no direction to consider because all point the same way.

His school colors are red and gold. His bruises are purple-black and blue, then green-plum, then a queasy yellow-green like thickfat sink-drain mucus. This is if he wins; his times never fast enough, take downs never quick enough.

**The entire school knows
you are a pussy.
Why are you such a girl? Put your fucking
dress on little girl.
Put it on
so I can give it to you
like I do your mother.**

It is a poem. It is a poem he memorizes. It is a poem he memorizes and will recite to many an unfortunate in the coming years.

He puts his dress on.

He receives.

Small, like his father, he knows he will never be able to win. He takes it as it is given, and when the sun comes out he enjoys its warmth for as long as it lasts which is never as long as he wishes it could be.

There is a bike that is built in those infrequent times of sun. It takes years to build it. When the bike is finally finished so is the son. He leaves its corpse in the garage before he goes, knowing its message will be lost on the man who helped him put it together.

There is no message he leaves for what was supposed to be his mother. His mother is a moth that has learned to love darkness.

I am not the first one he gets. The ones that come before me are crude and random. Birthed from the chaos of finding one's way, failed attempts at sign posts meant to guide but providing nothing. These early emblems paved with violence, drugs and drunk. These early emblems paving way for me. The one that's been with him always. The one he'd always been meant to carry.

I come on a clear day. One exactly like the one I will leave on. There is no breaking of waters, no contractions, just an internal knowing that propels him to the parlor where the two of us will finally be joined.

The vibrating needle's piercing rips the flesh away from me. It's a pain unlike any of the ones before, a fusion of torment and release. He grits his teeth together and takes it. Thinks of his father.

When it is over, the tattoo artist beams as if he had anything to do with my creation. All he did was peel back skin. Let me through.

What do you think?

The now-man steps to the mirror, turns sideways, takes me in. Our eyes meet and he knows and for the first and only time of his adulthood, he cries.

~ 4.
Today I Am A Genie

Today I am a genie. I am alone in a bottle. I am vapor waiting to become. It's been close to 25 years since the last time, 33 before that, before that 12 and on and on into that bottomless collecting vessel. This swirling energy. This potential, eager for release.

This is my place. That was what I was told. The words, a father's. Or that of a God. I am no longer sure. I only recall that the voice was deep. An internal thunder that commanded me. My turn had come and I transcended. A destiny shawl warm with duty.

I have been used many times and each time I provide. I have fulfilled every wish that fell within my boundaries. Poor to rich. Love lost to love found. Weak to strong. Ugly to beautiful. Sick to well. I am a maker of miracles. I am so very coveted. I am fulfiller of dreams. I *am* that of dreams. I am also the opposite. I am so very lonely. I am despair-choked inside a well of fetid darkness. I cannot pray enough for my undoing.

I do not feel the scratch of time but yet I feel a toll. Hundreds of years were but an evening. But thousands of hundreds of years wear one down. It's an ache within bones I do not often have. It is a murk that churns alongside me. My life is but a series of windows along a hallway that stretches eternal. I yearn for that glass, for those glimpses into what I've come to crave.

This is not an existence. I know that now. I used to believe it fulfilled me, that granting wishes was my duty, my purpose. Selfless. But time and time and time and time again and again watching the looks on their faces, their transformations, their gratitude for how I had changed them. I began to realize the imbalance. I began to yearn for some happiness of my own—the need for someone to hear me, listen and respond. The ache for more than an hour under sun or moon.

He has assured me not to worry, that my time will come. "Soon?" I ask. "Do not worry," he responds. "You will be released." It is a voice that resonates from nowhere. No comfort to be found in proximity. It's a purposeful distance. One I'm sure he created for just such a reason.

These words salve. They bring a peace that lasts for as long as I let them soothe. Their calm loosens a welcome rest from these ways I torture myself. Inside the bottle that sits wherever it endlessly sits, I trust. Blind and mute, I have no other choice.

After eons of this, after centuries upon centuries of every individual I have ever served dying their deaths, erasing whatever impact I had bestowed them, my confidence erodes. The anguish returns once more. With no form to assist me, I birth my own version of screaming. It is a cyclone that spins to madness. I do not know if he hears it, however I do not know how he cannot as I am told upon summoning how it was a faint wail that drew them to discover my bottle. How the pain it issued compelled them to find the source and shut it down. How it tore part of them loose in the process.

He *must* hear it but use equal strength to ignore it. Oh, the coldness!

When I am at my breaking he comes again and says again, "Do not worry." When I ask "Why not?" there is no answer other than the one he has given and given and given,

"You will be released."

I let it calm me. The screaming quiets. I wait for my next summoning. I try to hold on. I try to forget the embracing heat of a sun and the bright shine of a moon.

~ 5.
Today I Am A Niece

Today I am a niece. I have 3,333 uncles. I have 2,199 uncles. I might have 963 uncles. No, I have 744 uncles. I have 329 uncles or 75. Actually, I have 33. 33 uncles. I am lying. I have 6 uncles. I am still lying, I have 4. No. That's untrue. I have one uncle. One. That is the truth. It is true. One uncle. One uncle is enough to make me a niece. I don't need more than that. I just have the one. I was lying about all of the others. I have singular uncle. Not even an aunt. Not even 2 aunts or 47. Just the one uncle. He is like the Santa Claus of uncles because there is just one of him and there is just one Santa Claus and one God. But he is not the God of uncles which is why I didn't mention God before. He is my uncle. My only uncle.

My only uncle is dying right now or he is not. He's in a hospital right now or at least that's what he's telling me. I mean, I can't see him. He could be anywhere. During our phone conversation he said, "Doctor's here, can you hold on?" and he put the phone down and I could hear *doctor talk* so either it's an elaborate hoax executed by my one uncle for me to believe he's dying or he's not. He hasn't ever died yet though he should've been dead three times.

On the phone call from the (presumed) hospital bed

he asks me if I know the story of the first time he was supposed to be dead. Before I can answer he says he needs to tell me so I'll know the story when he's really dead and can then tell my children about it; their only great uncle who almost died three times. He tells me the story with a voice that sounds like it has a hole in it.

He's seven and he's sick. My grandpa, his dad, works at a market and never not works there. He's always there. Except for this day when he's for some reason home with my sick, seven year old uncle. It's a chance occurrence. It's pain in his seven year old stomach and it's just getting worse so my grandpa, his dad, takes him to the hospital where they discover his burst appendix. "The doctor came down the hallway shaking his head. He told my dad, your grandpa, if he'd waited fifteen minutes I'd be dead."

"Wow." I say.

"I shoulda been dead." He says.

"The second time I shoulda died...," he starts but the phone cuts in and out and there's no way I'm asking him to repeat it all because his voice sounds like it's been running uphill for thirty years. I presume he's telling me about something that happened when he had the throat cancer. Some tragic event I was told and forgot about. When he ends with, "...and that's the second time I shoulda been dead," I laugh and say, "Uncle, that's crazy!" even though I'm not really sure if it was. "I'm too stupid to die!" he says and now I wish I'd heard the story.

He says the third time is now. "I shoulda been dead!"

he says again. He sounds proud like he escaped death once more. His voice, however, sounds like it's standing behind him shaking its head. I ask him how the doctor says he's doing and he says his heart is only working at 25%. That sounds extremely bad to me but he seems unconcerned. "As soon as they figure out this heart thing they're gonna start me on the chemo." His throat cancer is back. He'd postponed his checkup until after football season and now he's dying or not dying. "I'm too stupid to die." He tells me that he needs to change his life; stop smoking, give up his Pepsis. He's also diabetic. My one and only uncle isn't good at doing what's good for him.

My lone uncle has only paid me two compliments my entire life. The first one was when I was 19. It was the first day of my first real job. He was visiting and had to borrow my car so he drove me to work. "You look very nice, except for those scuffed up shoes." The second time was when him and my mom were walking behind me through a parking lot in Las Vegas and he told me, "Your ass isn't as fat as it was before." My uncle isn't good at saying nice things.

Every time and I mean every time I call my uncle and he answers, "Hello?" I say, "Hi Unc! It's your favorite niece!" to which he replies, "You're my only niece." I am just now really realizing he is my only uncle.

We talk a bit more on the phone until the conversation winds completely down to bare threads. I feel like he's dying but he doesn't seem to feel the same way. I tell him to hang in there. To feel better. I tell him, "You can't die yet, you're my only uncle." "I know," he says.

"Okay, bye Unc. I love you."

"Same here," he says.My only uncle isn't good at saying nice things.

When he dies I will have zero uncles.

~ 6.
Today I Am A Salmon Trader

Today I am a salmon trader. Oh the bears! You think they can't swiftly run, but they can. They sprint! My success lies in the frequency with which I can keep the meat from their muzzles. Years of my body bloodied and torn with their valiant efforts. The meat is good. Worthy flesh that endlessly beckons. I cannot fault them. I've even had to train myself to hold fast from its calling. One cannot trade what one does not have.

I bring my meat to the mouths of men. All walks. None can resist. After they finger its deep pinkness; press their pads, discover its haughty resistance, smell its sweet promises, they are swooned. Money forced into my palms even before I've provided a price. "All of it" and "When can I get more" soon follow. It's a business that booms.

In the country, they come to me in the woods. Secret and huddled. It's one at a time. Nobody steps forward until the first one is gone. There is a patience among them that comes with a silent understanding of bottomless need. Each waits their turn, shifting their bodies anxious among the trees and brush. New animals so close to wounded prey. Our dealings always respectful; I never let them leave with less dignity than they came with. I do not flinch when their offerings cross over from monetary and useful to desperate; newborns, mouths and cunts of wives, daughters, servitude, I accept all reasonable offers. I have long since broken all boundaries. My lack of shame helps blind theirs.

In the city, none want to wait. There is no patience, only frenzy. They flood around my cart like the fish around my boots. I can only haul so much, I tell them as their curses come. The dealings are always fast. Silver bullets spraying from a gun. As their bags fill, so do mine. The cities are my hardest work but biggest payoff.

The colder the rivers, the more tender the fish. There's a way I loop them. Using ancient tools crafted by hands more torn than mine, I trap them. Wading into urgent waters that have taken me more times than I can count, I prepare the rounding. Letting out the snaking cordage, begging its spread disperses cleanly, covers evenly. Snares and tangles among the defeats I am prone to suffer. Their undoing is potentially mine. Risking myself again and again for this life I have chosen.

I am accustomed to being cold and wet. I believe my bones and muscles are different than most. Over the years of frigid soaking, they've adapted. Some sort of added bonding between them that insulates. A pairing they've wed like lovers. Or maybe they just conspire in blinding me to the pain. Either way, I am thankful something is saving me.

The fish flock as birds. After my tendrils have spread and the waiting has pressed taut against the breast of claiming, they come. They always come. I sing a song of destiny that draws them. The words explain that this is the moment they were meant for. It harrows a point of truth within them that explodes and they swim at me like I'm a beacon. It's a homecoming. I stand in the rushing water as they gather around me, frenzied. This is the point of exhilaration. The silver bodies crowding around me, so urgent to find what they have been called to. The more they don't find, they more crazed they become. I stand with my song booming, a pillar among them, my heartbeat matching their wet flapping. I hold that moment as long as I can, savoring. All the while vigilant for the crafty bears that have begun to learn the song for themselves. When I am on the cusp of crossing over with the need to join them, I act. I spring the webbing and it blossoms around them like a dust cloud, traps them tight and closes down. Their clamor ceases and I feel their longing turn to black.

I am not ignorant of their sadness. I feel it too. I let it weigh me. I let it disperse.

Then I drag the fish for trading.

~ 7.
Today I Am A Slave

Today I am a slave. Pepito tried to drown me again. My face right down to the fishes before I sprung out of it. Came out sputtering. He just stood there staring at me, all dark to his calves, panting like he'd finished a too-vigorous laugh. I whipped my head fast and quick. My hair flapped and stuck to the back of my head. It made the greatest sound. "It's fucking freezing. What the fuck?" I said.

We went home and I made him sandwiches. He likes ham and cheese and also tuna melts. The ham and cheeses always have to be cut on the diagonal, the tuna, open-faced. I get whatever he leaves. Those aren't cut any way at all.

He was the last slave. When he conquered and took over, he found me, and now I am the slave.

I lie in his lap. "Am I a good slave?"

"You are the best slave."

He uses different hairbrushes on me. Never knew there were so many different kinds of hairbrushes.

Pepito makes me take baths. They are very hot and I am in them until their volume turns down to cold. I sit and stare at the moon photo on the wall. The frame only has three sides. Every time I ask him if he would like me to fix it, he says he likes it that way.

He likes imperfect things.

I have three nipples.

After the bath he usually has me speak to his children. I wear the mask he made and get on Skype. I ask his son how his game was and if the coach let him play. His son responds with things he would tell anybody. Sometimes I don't even know what he's saying. Like his words are Easter egg dye all spinning down a flushing toilet. I ask his daughter how gymnastics was and she tells me about the slumber party she went to where all of the girls pretended to fix her pretty with make-up but instead made her look like a clown and how they made her drink water that had been dipped with a bloody tampon and how they all called her "Fat Sarah" and how she cried and locked herself in the bathroom until everything got quiet and even past that when it became emptiness. I wanted to tell her about my nipples but I didn't. I cried beneath the mask and after I disconnected I folded and ironed all of Pepito's laundry.

Except for trying to kill me every day, Pepito is pretty nice. He's definitely getting better at it though. Surprising me now, but I am vigilant. I don't want to die and I don't think he wants to kill me. Yet. After he comes close, he tells me, "One day you will conquer. One day you will have a slave of your own. And so on." Like he's trying to make me feel better. It's encouraging.

~ 8.
Today I Am A Short Order Cook

Today I am a short order cook. You won't watch *The Dark Knight Rises* with me. Friday you wouldn't watch it with me. Saturday you wouldn't watch it with me. Sunday you wouldn't watch it with me. Also, Monday you wouldn't watch it with me. None of the days you watched it with me.

But still I made you pancakes. The morning you slept all hungry in the bed, I heard your stomach. I knew even before you did what your body wanted.

You woke up, pissed, and followed that smell all the way up front. What did you find? You found me; free-range breasts under my sleep shirt, my black baby hairs all greasy-steam twists swing-bouncing against my face like chandelier crystals, all my legs—thighs to toes—feet hugged in thick, slouchy gray socks—old grandpas. The whole of it suggesting I can still be pretty so early, so unkempt.

You found me, those fucking pancakes, and their friends, the sausages. What did you say then?

"We got any juice?"

But no *Dark Knight Rises*. But I can cook some bacon cheeseburgers. Some Philly cheesesteaks. I can French fry like a motherfucker. I can scrape scrape scrape burnt cheese from hot silver with my loyal steed, Spatula. All the while my skin layering up the grease, frosted-cake thick. All the while you couch, you garage, you sleep and lean.

All the while I am adding another yellow armpit t-shirt to my collection of hundreds.

Now you are locked in a room, listening to jazz. There has never been any jazz before. None in all the days. It's loud and seems loose-pretty. I can't hear very well through the sizzle.

I don't know what's happening anymore.

I flip the hash browns, the bacon and ready the eggs. If you won't watch *Dark Knight Rises* with me tonight, I don't know what I'll do.

Probably pace in this kitchen until I die.

Or find a different one.

~ 9.
Today I Am A Wife

Today I am a wife. My husband and I are watching *American Ninja* which is a rip-off of a Japanese competition show where run of the mill people try out to be ninjas. A young male contestant just peeled off a clingy yellow jumpsuit, revealing a half-naked, tan, muscled body. I sighed audibly in a pathetic, giving-up sort of way which resulted in a grunt from my husband. His grunts mean many things and I can usually interpret them, although this time I couldn't. But that doesn't really matter. Who cares?

This morning I felt pretty enthusiastic and thought I would make some pancakes but there was only a half cup of Bisquick left in the box. I thought, Good thing I didn't tell him I was going to make pancakes because now there's one less thing he can be disappointed in me for. I made steel-cut oatmeal instead. He said it didn't have enough honey so I brought it back to the kitchen and gave it one more squirt. I looked into the plastic bear's eyes before setting it down and I told it, "Squirt, squirt, squirt, Ann."

Today was Sunday and I woke up not feeling so good. I kept this to myself because it doesn't matter. Who inhabits my body? Answer: me. This means it's my business. "Your body, your business, Ann!"

I wanted to take a nap but I took some Airborne instead. I had too many things to do today. "Things to do, Ann! People to see!!"

There were some new action movies that opened on Friday, so after I was done getting the cars washed and doing the groceries, I got to pick which one we were going to go to. "Lady's choice, Ann!" Lucky me. I still really wanted to take a nap but we were already planning to go see a movie so that was the plan and you always have to stick with the plan. "Always stick with the plan, Ann!"

I tried to nap during the movie but there were too many gunshots and explosions. This didn't seem a problem for my husband. At least that meant more popcorn for me.

Before the movie, in the parking lot, he saw I was wearing my yellow Lakers jersey t-shirt and he goes, "Better watch out, Ann, people are going to think you are a Laker girl!" And then he started laughing hysterically. It *was* pretty funny, though. Ha. He's full of jokes like that.

I've just decided I'm going to hit the hay. I'm sick and tired. So sick and tired. I'm going to leave him here in front of *American Ninja*. Some black guy with a red bandana is in the lead and I don't care who wins. I'll leave the bedroom door cracked so I can hear the television because I want to masturbate before I sleep and I don't want him coming in and ruining it all. I'm going to think about the young man in the yellow jumpsuit. I'll be there on the set of *American Ninja*. He's going to notice me in the crowd with my bright yellow Lakers jersey. He'll head straight for me and ask if I am a Laker Girl. Then, after I shake my head, giggle and demur, "That's none of your business," he'll look me up and down and then say something like, "I'd like to make your *body* my business." Then he'll take my hand and we'll go behind some enormous climbing apparatus and he'll make love to me soft and then hard. He won't call me Ann and all of his grunts will mean the same thing; "You are wanted."

~ 10.
Today I Am A Whore

Today I am a whore. But it's only because a meteor is about to hit the earth. It's the size of El Capitan. Every scientist is in agreement on this one. Every trajectory measurement points to impact. The end of the world as we know it. For real this time.

I wasn't a whore two weeks ago. Only since this meteor business. Only in the past 5 days.

My husband is kind of mad that I'm a whore now. I'm like, "Sorry, Bob. It's been a faithful 24 years and all, but it's time for me to get some new dick." He's like, "Fuck, Angela! This should be the time we pull together as a family! Hold each other. Remember all that we've had, what we've been through, how much we love each other. Not go out in a fucking pile of sweat and cum! Think of the kids!"

But, I'm all, "Sorry, Bob." And then I drive to any bar in any city in any town in any country that exists and fuck everyone there. I fuck Chinese guys, Tahitian guys, Argentinian guys, Canadian guys, French-Canadian guys, Irish guys, Filipino guys, Japanese guys, German guys, Haitian guys, Russian guys and guys from Philadelphia. I fuck guys from Brazil, the

Congo, Iceland, The Netherlands, Zimbabwe, Sweden, England, Greece, Thailand, Italy, South Korea, India, Vietnam and Brooklyn. I also fuck a bunch of ladies, bartenders, a mature twelve year old, two large dogs and a man claiming to be an extra-terrestrial.

Bars no longer have tables and chairs, only mattresses and tons of sheets and towels. All the stools and tables have been piled out in front of the bars like a pyre waiting to happen. Most have already happened. Our cities look like the meteor has already touched down. It's frightening.

When I am too sore from all the fucking I leave whatever bar I'm in and go home. The first thing I do when I squint into the day or moonlight, fresh air on my sticky-slick skin, is stare up into the sky and look for the meteor. So far nothing. The sky sits clear and innocent. But they assure us it's there and it's only a matter of days.

I go home to Bob and the kids.

I shower and sleep and the next day he begs me to stay again.

Again, I do not.

~ 11.
Today I Am A Bulimic

Today I am a bulimic. I take in the world. I throw it up.
Do you want to see pain? Hold on for a minute. Just
one minute. That's all it takes for me to work it back
up. Do you have patience? Are you a patient person?
The one who waits the longest gets the best payoff.
Please trust me.

The last thing I ate was my back fat. I paid a young
neighbor, a young man, to come over my house and
slice it off for me. He'd done similar before. He brought
the belt again. He brought the knife. He helped me
into the tub. He was quick.

Again.

It's unbelievable how much I can swallow. An ongoing
gorging since I was a girl: Frosted Flakes, a handful of
bow shaped barrettes, twelve ice creams, seven fingers
of my brothers' friends inside me, my grandmother's
homemade pesto sauce, a 12" bass, 17 crawdads with
melted butter, 147 Ritz crackers with Velveeta slices
melted on them, 7 pounds of Rice A Roni (chicken fla-
vor), a naked, sunbathing neighbor, 89 peanut butter
and jelly sandwiches, my dad kicking my brother up
to his room 13 times, 67 gallons of cherry Kool Aid, 14

years of being 'the fat friend', 18 refrigerator magnets from all the places my mom would go to after the divorce, so many French fries, how many hamburgers, an entire truck bed of ranch dressing, the fat guy with the mustache in the back seat that started this entire mess, whipped cream filled pie pans, some fruits and vegetables, enough beef ribs to forge a canyon, peanut butter filled private parts and the animals that came to empty them, 32 avocados disguised as human hearts, 12 pounds pork and chicken adobo, 6 football fields of white rice, my dad my dad my dad, how I'm not good enough never good enough and infinity times I avoid looking in the mirror.

My belly is as big as all the tomorrows.

I am good at it now. I wasn't in the beginning. It only takes 47 seconds. Or 58. Or 71. It only takes long enough for me to not care how long it takes. The time it takes doesn't matter. What matters is how you feel afterwards.

Here's what you do:

1. Eat enough to make you feel sick and/or hate yourself.

2. Hide yourself in the bathroom. Make it a cocoon.

3. Cover everything in cotton. Anything that could make you feel more shame than you already do.

4. Approach the toilet. Make sure it hasn't been cleaned in a while. The filth will help you.

5. Spread your legs. Twirl your hair into a tube. Tuck that tube into your shirt.

6. Take a deep breath.

7. Stare at the toilet water. Feel how gross you are, how utterly disgusting and worthless you are.

8. Restrain yourself from licking the shit and piss stains from the porcelain. Imagine it instead.

9. If this imagery isn't already making you puke, use your fingers. Take two of them and reach beyond your tonsils.

10. If this doesn't make you puke, reach further. Reach all the way into your stomach. Reach as far as you can.

11. After each hurl reach again. Keep fucking puking. Empty your fucking guts. Remember to

breathe. Remember you are a big piece of shit.

12. Don't wipe the tears and snot until you are done. Or don't wipe them at all. Sometimes it's nice to leave them there and just sit cross-legged in front of the mirror staring at how fucking ugly you are.

13. Lie back on the tile and let its cool try to make you feel better.

14. Stop crying.

15. Flush.

It's so easy. So fucking easy.

Do it every day.

Let it become your life.

~ 12.
Today I Am A Babysitter

Today I am a babysitter. So overweight. So plump. A landscape of skin. You leave everything I need in the freezer, in the refrigerator, in the cupboards, on the shelves. "Don't hide the wrappers," you tell me. "I want to know everything that's making you more."

"She dresses horrible. Such a pretty girl too, it's a shame. Kids today..." Your wife doesn't like how I wear too-tight things. How my low-rise jeans and too-small t-shirts let my gut escape, all forced between the fabrics and exploded. You love the fishbelly-white skin, how it's a beacon for you.

"I'm hardly a kid," I complain.

"Never mind her," you say. "Wear what you wear."

I do.

I come over as arranged; one hour before you need to leave for the theater. Your wife likes little Mandy to be slowly acclimated to my presence; like placing a frog in a pot of water and turning on the burner. Little Mandy needs to adapt to me in a way that is seamless. Your wife wants the both of you to be able to leave without little Mandy making a scene. She wants to be able to slip away with you without little Mandy even realizing.

It's what you, in turn, do to your wife. The half a sleeping pill you slip into her tea when I arrive at the house. The way you get her comfortable in the theater seats, making sure to take away any popcorn she might be holding before she nods off. The quiet way you leave her side, rushing out of the theater to the car, then to me, then back again. The way you return, slipping silently beside her just as the credits begin to roll, then playfully chastising her about falling asleep, *again*.

Seamless.

You are a clever, clever boy, always choosing movies with the longest running times. With the theater a mere 6 minutes away from the house and the absence of mid-morning traffic, we usually have a good 90-112 minutes together. I get naked as soon as I get your text. It's always the same, "Is little Mandy ok?"

Clever, clever boy.

I spread myself on the couch, the way you like me. The maniacal look on your face as you drop your keys on the kitchen table, the way you make your way to my flesh, hands Frankenstein-forward, eyes fat-riveted as if nothing else exists, not even me, is my favorite moment every time.

You dive into me, face first. Your mouth and nose pushing air out against me until noise ripples out in absurd flatulence-like bursts. Your tongue soon follows, heavy with slobber, sliming over every fold you are busy squeezing into entirely new appendages. It only takes a few minutes for the wet to mix with the air, changing the farty outbursts into wet, undulating rumbles.

I let you knead and rub as much as you want, as hard as you want. Even on the days when your arthritis is absent and it hurts; the new found strength in your hands a punishment taken out on my rolls. You'll be proud of the bruises later. "Makes me feel like a young man seeing that," your fingers tracing paths over the purple-blue.

Little Mandy will jump up on us sometimes. Her fur getting soaked in your drool. We'll laugh and you'll lift her, scolding, "No, no, little Mandy!" while placing her back down on the floor.

You go back to your wife, then both of you come back to me. Snacks are eaten between the three of us while we discuss the movie and what little Mandy was up to during it. You both decide to see another senior early-bird showing two days from now and you tell me you'll text me what time I'm needed. I take the money you give me and go back home. I have just enough time to rotate the laundry before having to pick up my daughter from school. We stop at McDonald's on the way home.

~ 13.
Today I Am A Basketball Coach

Today I am a basketball coach. I hear the parents' voices. All of the hands grasping and shaking me. Wanting me to come back. Begging me. I cannot. It's nice here, under this table. With my eyes closed, it's almost dark. I wish I could ask someone to turn off the gym lights. Paint black the skylights. I want to yell, "Leave me alone! Please! Just leave me alone!" but I know I am crazy enough right now. I don't need to take it further. But if I am shaken one more time...

I have collapsed. I cannot continue. My knees will not unbend. They could, but I will not ask them to. I will leave my legs alone. Such fragile things. China. Eggshells. Windowpanes.

What they do not know is what they cannot see. It's what *I* can see. What I can't *stop* seeing. Hearing. It's all of their sons screaming in unison. It's white shards making themselves known. Shooting proud through their earth of flesh, overeager to see the sky first hand; a fantastic thing told to them before bedtime, perhaps. Painted excessively magical, overly beautiful. Something fabled they needed to make true. For themselves, their sanity.

I see the boys writhing. Their skins so different, yet, in pain, the same. In blood and bone, the same. Anything that falls below the break lies separate, askew, or dangling. Nothing below the break makes sense. They are just dead things that used to be. They are my childhood home after my mother got the phone call that made her unable to stop scream-crying for hours and then days. They are my brother lying in his casket, the crushed half of him hidden under the closed half-lid. They are my brother's empty bed my parents refused to remove from my room. They are things you need to carry on from. Things you must "make the best of." Things useless now they are apart from what they belonged to.

In my dreams the paramedics leave them there, the broken alphabet of limbs strewn across a Pollock of blood. The parents, having hysterically followed the lights and sirens to care for their sons, leave me alone to clean the mess. I grab a push broom. I pile them. A soft kindling of expensive sneakers, red-soaked sweat socks, and skin fuzzed with hair still too young to have understood they would soon have belonged to a man.

I cannot get out from where I am. I cannot bear to see them jump even one more time. I will stay curled. I will keep their sons whole.

~ 14.
Today I Am A Farmer

Today I am a farmer. Everything I grow is dying. There's a window upstairs where she watches. I keep my smile on. I wave into the sun, squinting. She's dying too; she doesn't need more worry from me.

When I see the stalks are right, I pull them. Each time thinking, *this time will be different*. This time I'll see an intact casing with a hue even and full. I'll be able to swing them into the bed with confidence, trusting they'll make a hard thud against the others; a sound indicative of unripeness, a thick promise of rewards to come. I'll be able to work a fruitful morning before the heat of the sun becomes unbearable with the coming noon. I'll be able to haul my bounty into the cool of the shed, go in and make lunch, sit with her without fret. Just a regular day with a regular crop.

But it never is.

So many things happen when I pull the stalks. I find myself bracing. There is a clench in my chest and jaw. I suck my breath. I think a quick segment of prayer. A section of words God should be familiar with. I tighten the part of me that threatens to collapse into despair and fear. All of this takes place in the moment before the pull.

When the pull happens, there is a natural release that comes with the process. Taking something out of something else using force has an inherent satisfaction. They way it holds then relents. How it lets go into you; a type of giving. So, there is that feeling, but it is false. It is a trick. The pleasure is as fleeting as a sneeze.

With the pull comes the disgust. Which variation will be hanging off the green in my fist? None of them the same, yet all of them bulbous and dripping. All of them with a fecal, rotting stench. The fleshy, oozed gapings exposing further, internal horrors.

How many wounds can I pull from the earth?

I want to hurl each one of them. I want to build a pyre and feed them into it. But I cannot. I have no choice but to toss them into the truck bed, hear the wet slap and gurgled cries as they join the growing pile. She is watching from the window. She must see nothing different.

The harvest squirms. My mind screams.

Is screaming.

I pull swiftly through the morning, wanting to rid my field of this blight as quickly as I can. The sun is hotter today. I will dump this load next to the one from the previous day, which sits next to the one from the day before which sits next to the one from the day before that. All of them outside the shed, away from the view from her window. I pray the sun has finally burned their wet away, dried them dead. I cannot bear to hear their mewling anymore, the moist squelch of their struggling.

If I know they can die, I know I can be rid of them. I can clear my field and start anew. I can go to her with peace in my heart and tell her everything is just fine and she will smile at me in her new weak way that will make me almost believe it.

~ 15.
Today I Am A Caretaker

Today I am a caretaker. I have to be careful now that my son is watching. You live what you learn, they say, so I'm extra gentle. I need to make sure he learns how to treat me when *I'm* old and exploding.

I narrate my motions.

"I'm opening the drapes now so she can see and feel the warm sunlight. Keep the sheers closed though, because you don't want her get blinded if she opens her eyes."

"See how softly I'm speaking? It lets her know I'm here in a way that feels like a voice hug. It spreads a calm inside of her."

"Pull the wheelie-tray table over to the foot of the bed. Make sure it has everything you need and all of it is unwrapped and sterilized."

"Now, pull the covers back slowly. All the way. One even motion. Pretend you're uncovering a pond of sleeping frogs."

My mother lies sleeping through all of this, or lies quiet

and away in whatever bottomless place she's resting in.

It's hard to tell without measuring if her leg is larger than it was yesterday. Even so, I know that it is. It's growing faster than a seedling, but just as undetectable. If I had some sort of high-speed camera filming it, I could play it back and see it swelling.

I lift her nightgown up over her knees. My son shifts on the bed, sits up. He knows the important part is about to come.

"Hand me the long scissors," I say, and he does.

"Slide it between the bandage and her skin. Be very, very careful. Pretend her leg is a water balloon filled with lava."

I cut the bandage from shin to toe.

"Now I lift her leg up by the ankle. Her heel's in my palm. See?"

As I lift, the bandage sort of slides off and flaps open. It's the color and weight of an overused Kleenex. There is a bottom of a river smell. My son holds his nose and squinches his face. I do my best to not react. I rub the water that is coming from my eyes on my sleeve.

"If you whistle, it might help," I tell him. "With the smell," I add. Somebody told me this helps when cutting onions. I'm not sure if it helps an eight year old with the smell of his grandmother's exploding leg, but at the least it would be distraction.

Fascinated, he gives several earnest pursed blows that emit nothing remotely musical.

"I don't know how to," he confesses, wistfully.

"Well, guess that's something we can work on shortly, then, can't we?"

He nods and smiles. I scoop the used dressing and place it in a plastic grocery bag, drop it on the floor.

"Come closer."

I let him watch me wash, clean and apply medicine to her leg. I hum while I work. In my head the hum is a song that has words.

*"Do you see, my son, how I am washing every bit of this disgusting leg? Are you hearing my carefree humming? Is it painting a picture of composure? Look at how I dab the meaty broccoli-like bulbs that are pushing their way through her now purple-brown skin. I am not even biting my lip or squinting my eyes. I am actively touching their yellowy-red spongy surfaces with these cotton balls covered in medicine. Can you feel the obscene heat of this expanding leg? Like it is an overheating radiator? Look at how I am not disgusted with my own mother and her leg that is expanding and splitting apart at the speed of life. Look at what love is. Can you see, my son, that love is ruining three mattress pads with your mother's leg leakings? That love is humming while touching things you want to run away from? Are you learning, my son? Will our positions be shifted one far away day? Will you be the one humming while parts of **me** explode?*

Will you have taught your son to whistle?"

~ 16.
Today I Am A Hunchback

Today I am a hunchback. Across the wall, the sound of a baby crying. I wonder which fence it's coming over. I wonder why still, in my resting, I am sought out. An intelligent missile, they won't even let me have the peace of a quiet morning!

Babies are cruel. Wrapped in the guise of under-development and newborn cute, they always escape this deserved accusation. Everybody looks past their evil. Even when they are hands-covered in their soupy, foul shit. Even when they are piss-wet and puke doused. Even after night after night of their little beasts keeping them awake with their screaming. Their greatest torture to feign peaceful slumber, counting ever so giddily to 1,000 then wailing once again, even stronger, waking the greedy, sleep-whored birthers.

Innocents, my warted ass!

But I am distracted. The morning wails set me off-course. Such an eventful night! My stomach wrought with sick once more! Up, intermittently, until dawn. Vacating waste from my opposite holes. A violent usurpation of my wet, twisted guts! I am spent with its wrenching!

It is no other's fault than my own. My body; a garbage dump of my intake. The "food" I am thrown by the peasants, albeit oftentimes tolerable, is often rotted, or on its way to rot. I rarely discern. In my pen, I am in constant hunger. My hump needs feeding and I am pressed to fulfill its compulsion or suffer more.

I can see the way my sick grows. My stomach, the well of a toilet, shat into by all. Its depth piling and piling with every variety of shits and pisses. Mounting higher and higher until its filth peaks above the rim.

That is my innards.

That is my guts.

It revolts in the night.

The days I am viewed, I unleash my anger. My frustrations over this body I've been given. The pain and trouble it's provided since my unfortunate birth. My keepers have doubled the moat, raised my bars, set the crowd back to ensure their safety. Such a satisfaction!

I focus on the children. My ambition; to fill them with the darkest of nightmares. Ones they will then render upon their parents. In this way, I am no longer hovelled in this pen, I am running free, spreading my revenge for their cruelty into their very bed chambers. I may be a beastly-thing, but my mind is sharp. One day, they will know. One day they will wish they had never kept me.

~ 17.
Today I Am A Victim

Today I am a victim. Last night, I dreamt of spiders. A melted cheese of them pouring over. A thousand scabies that fell against, then inside of me, tiny bitter bitings. A wearing away. My skin tightened and caved. Buckled. I woke not screaming, but shaken.

Everything blue then blackened. Like burning, but softer. Collapsing.

A sodden roof.

In the daylight, I decided to be brave. Forget the spiders. Forget the fear. What I was touching, THAT was what was real. Nothing eating me away. Nothing taking all the small bits of me until they became large chunks. No. In this bright exposure, I was just me; wearing a gray t-shirt, new ballet shoes that rubbed raw my virgin heels, my blotchy skin, my unconfidence. All of the incompetence. All of the failing. How it screamed. THAT was real. A touchstone.

I made my way in the light. Lookit my feathers. Lookit my fangs. All tapered. Nothing sharp. I waltzed, feeling all the predators predating me. Hunched and ready behind every boulder, robust and waiting to pounce. I

was their dancer. Their ballerina. Their ready victim.
My blunted paws retarded and useless. Such a fakery.
How they took me.

How I let them.

How I let them,

Still.

~ 18.
Today I Am A Failure

Today I am a failure. Nobody wants me. They say they do,

Then...

Let's start at the beginning, hashtag, let's not. The failure is starting to like drinking too much again, but, to err is human, to forgive let's look at dads and how, when they turn gray it makes you forget, how they get smaller when their fingers dig into the dirt of gardens. Remember wine coolers, though? How the bottles stabbed so sweet once the panties were pushed aside? Hey Bartles! Hey James! It's like a threesome.

Take the failure to lunch. Hey, I know! There's this little street I pissed in an alley behind. It's cobbled, like with bricks, not cobbles what are those and do they exist. The street is like a movie set. It's where I feel almost safe enough to punch out every window with my fists and face. Sugar panes. You can take me to a place where the food is Mexican and the walls are covered in Elvis memorabilia. Every inch, an Elvis. I want a carousel horse with Xmas bells hanging where its balls should be. I want it dangling from the ceiling of this place. I want to eat under it, with you. Elvis music

Elvis movies playing to us like we are underneath an Elvis merry go round. Let's have wet cake. Let's eat all the free chips and ask for more.

The failure made a God box. It's squarish and half-wrapped with gold paper like a little girl dipped it in paint then forgot about it because her dad came home LOUD. The God box has a slit to swallow the failure's fears. The fears are made with dates. Made with begs and pleases. The fears are made with Bics. Folded and shoved in like suppositories. The failure thinks this will help, but she's wrong. They're only busting the walls of the box. The sound it makes when they are slipped in is hearty laughter. The little girl runs back to dip the rest of her box but her hands won't stop shaking and the paint is dry. She will wait forty years to make it again.

The failure is only good at two things: One, you can make money but you lose your soul in the process; the other is where she puts her soul but, so far, it doesn't pay much.

Maybe one day.

~ 19.
Today I Am Unemployed

Today I am unemployed. So far, every day feels like a Saturday. Yesterday while I was driving around in the middle of the morning running errands something felt wrong. It felt like I forgot something. I kept looking down to make sure I was wearing pants.

Reality is weighted, heavy. It is an anvil tied to the all of you, pulling you down. Extra gravity. At night it turns to locusts. A tiny, swarm with equal heft. They nest inside the mind. They are a wriggling, restless mass. They don't let you sleep.

Last night I brought shit into the bed. I smelled it everywhere but I didn't do anything and he didn't notice.

In the morning, I found shit on my elbow and on my wrist. I untucked the fitted sheet and folded it over the smears so the maid wouldn't see.

Last night was a living, awake, nightmare. The kind where when you wake up from not really being asleep, it is still there.

Tomorrow is Saturday.

I wonder if it will feel like Thursday.

~ 20.
Today I Am An Outlier

Today I am an outlier. It's very cerebral to watch your menstrual blood stretch out of your body. I say stretch, because it's not a pouring. It's not a flood. It's the peacefulness of a fishbowl and the serenity of a koi pond. The liquid is dense. It has a strength to it. Reminds me of the Incredible Hulk after he's been smashed to bits by a bigger, tougher foe. An ugly thing clinging to its strength while it lies useless.

My period blood is made for bigger things. It's an important liquid made waste when not called upon. It's like the genie from the lamp giving up and leaving, bags slung over shoulder, after eons of nobody rubbing.

I sat many times today, staring at the space between my crotch and the toilet water just watching blood leave my body. Again, it's a stretching. Like a snot-filled length of saliva. Like cold honey.

When it hits the water, it becomes Easter egg dye. It blooms and sinks. It's serenity, I'm telling you! I was mesmerized. There were thin strings, sharp and intent. Glossy. Then, thicker cords, still slim but bulky; business-minded. Clumps. Tiny ones, nothing embryo-sized. Let's not get gross here. The clumps were respectful. I wanted to salute them. I might've done just that. I might've saluted a few of my period blood clumps. So what?

I have a lot of stress right now. I didn't mean to stare at my dripping menses all afternoon, okay. It just happened. It brought me some momentary peace.

Have you ever been so stressed out you just wanted to walk and walk and walk until.... The until is the part I wanted to get to. Like, what would happen? What is the "until?" Shitting my pants? My legs collapsing? My feet wearing down to the bone?

I am starting to understand the time my mother lost her mind and had to go to the hospital. The time she gave us silver dollars for the ice cream truck and made us burn all the cartons of cigarettes in the fireplace.

Do you think I could get a job as a Disney princess? Yeah, I'd be a fat and ugly version of whatever princess but, I could totally fake the kindness. I just want to wear those dresses, ya know? Spin round and round like I'm what they want me to be? I just want to smear an entire tube of red lipstick around and around my lips until I look like I belong in a straightjacket.

"Am I pretty?"

My boss cried in my office today. Our most expensive costume got ruined after SHE RENTED IT WITHOUT HAVING THEM SIGN THE INSURANCE PAPERS!!! And we all know that is a no-no in the costume rental business, now, don't we?

She was all, "Malibu! Malibu! What am I going to do now?!" She was worried about the owner who was going to for sure fire her.

I just shrugged my shoulder and was all, "LinkedIn, baby."

My husband hasn't been home in two days. I keep hearing helicopters flying over my house. Where are my kids? I've been eating out of the same bowl for a week now. I have a shelf full of Ken's Steakhouse Dressing. I bought off-brand cornflakes. There is no money left in the emergency account. I have started praying again.

I wanted to tell you something else but now I've forgotten it. I am filled with fleeting thoughts. I want my head to be a microwave sometimes. I want my head to be an explosion of better things to come.

~ 21.
Today I Am A Time Machine

Today I am a time machine. My little brother is my operator. There is a power switch beneath every scar I bear, visible and invisible. Even though he's created me, he doesn't know about all the switches. He just knows about the ones he knows about and the ones he thinks I know about. The rest of the switches, the scars, are all secrets.

My little brother drinks Budweiser all day, every day. Morning until night. He brushes his teeth with it, makes his coffee with it then showers with it. Just kidding. My brother never takes showers. He swims in rivers, considers it a cleansing. But the Budweiser... I can't see my brother without red, white and blue fists. Hammer-ends against his face, against his face, against his face. All day, the hammering, the getting hammered. And, like footprints, everywhere, the cans. They keep track of where he goes, where he's been. An aluminum history.

He uses me at night, when his face is most bruised, when the cans are so high they trap us both, otherwise, I'd leave. I never wanted to be this for him...this time machine. But he insists.

The word he uses to flip each switch is, "remember," then it is a running downhill. Those grassy hillsides that slant at such an incline to make stopping impossible. He asks, "Remember...?" and then words come out that I am forced to hear and because I am programmed, I must respond. This is part of the deal. It's why he made me this.

He presses so many switches.

"Remember...?" "Remember...?" "Remember...?" "Remember...?" "Remember...?" "Remember...?"

"Remember...?" "Remember...?" "Remember...?" "Remember...?" "Remember...?" "Remember...?"

If I don't, he always does. The stories unbury everything. So many tales of stupidity and risk. I struggle in his telling. In my own. I know most every story, and the ones I don't, he insists at. In his remembering, the sky is a constant blue. The sun, shining. His eyes turn to glass as he recounts, like he is looking into the away. His mouth a wistful grin. "Remember...?" And I do. But differently. And more. I think, because he was so much younger. So behind me he didn't see. My girlhood, a stone in the river ahead of him, obstructing the rapids up ahead.

My eyes are also glass. My mouth less wistful. Old now, I question why were we allowed such summer lives? How were we so lucky? Why were we—why was I—left to be so unlucky? Why were we left to dry in the wind?

I am pained. The switches that only I can press are the ones that activate the memories he doesn't know about. The ones nobody knows about. The ones where I was little girl prey. Pecked and pecked at each summer. Small sections removed in quick, precise stabbings. Colandered.

While my switches whirr and my circuitry begs to shut down, the wall of cans builds around us. My brother's nostalgic yearning of times spent better than now is betrayed by his aluminum cocoon. How much has he buried? How much has he hammered down with his patriotic fists?

"Remember...?" and then he says my name. And I remember. Which means things were real. Which means the other things were real too. The things *I've* hammered down.

He has made me his time machine so he can stay there. He tells me this. He wants me to open myself wide enough that he can crawl through. Go back to the boy he once was. In the summers, when he couldn't see much more than right in front of him. Back to when his life wasn't as tarnished as it is now. Back to when his fists were that of a little boy, flesh-colored and fingered.

I want to tell him we can't go back. That we can only visit, or choose to forget.

But that's not in my programming.

~ 22.
Today I Am A Lion

Today I am a lion. My little brother is a lion. We are lions together. We roam the woods behind our house until our footpads bleed. Lots of hunting but also playing and sleeping. There are mostly squirrels so we have to hunt a LOT because our stomachs are so big and the squirrels are so small. Once in a while there is a bunny or a raccoon. Not much heartier. I turn back into a boy to shoot them with my BB gun. Each time I kill one, my brother roars. I become a lion again and we go rip it apart with our teeth. Blood smears our chins, our short manes.

Our mother's favorite color is roses. When I was the only cub, they were everywhere. All around the yard. I'd pet their petals with my paws, lost in their scent. "Why are there so many, mommy?" "Because they're my favorite color," she'd say. Then she'd chase me all around the roses, pouncing and pouncing until she'd catch me. Her paws so giant they'd eat up my chest. I had nowhere else to go but my back against the grass. My growls turned into that of a boy's laughter and hers into a mother's. When we both tired, she'd pick me up by my scruff, her fierce mouth soft against my fur, and carry me into our den where we'd curl together and nap until our father came home from his hunting. His muzzle dried bloody from the kill, carcass heavy and dragging.

My little brother doesn't know our mother's favorite color. The roses all died after our father didn't come back from the hunt. He'd been in her belly the entire time and never was able to see them.

"But what about when she'd roar?" I asked, "Couldn't you see then?"

"No. I was sleeping."

"How did you sleep with so much roaring?" I asked. My mother's roars were deafening. I remember putting my head into my paws to drown it out.

After our father didn't come back my mother couldn't stop roaring. It was all she did. That's when our play ended. That's when our den went rotten. That's when the roses died. I tried to save them at first. I gathered their mottled bodies from the ground with my boy hands and brought them to her, hoping it would stop her roars.

I stood inside her hot breath, inside the bottomless sound that kept pushing out of her. "Look mommy, your favorite color!"

It took many times to make myself heard. When she finally ceased her roar I felt a hope spark inside of me. We stood there together for a minute in the new silence her roar had left. The den fell away and our house stepped forward. I could see the squashed couch again. The carpet with all the rips and spills. I could even smell the awful from the kitchen. It felt like a waking up. All of a sudden, I didn't want it. I wanted to push it back. But it was too late.

I could see her face want to change for a minute. Her fur thinned to skin and back. Her eyes blurred between gold and blue. Her muzzle retracted then lengthened, teeth sabered then squared, ears sliding from the top of her head down the sides and then returning. The two parts of her fighting for what world she wanted to belong to.

She never came back.

My brother and I walk both worlds. We have to. Our mother is stuck as a lion and we are lions but we are also boys. We still need the things of man.

Ever since my brother was a cub I've had to teach him the ways of both livings. I start him early on the hunt. Earlier than even I had as now we are our only hunters. His approaches are rough at first and he is scared and timid, but as he ages he learns and we triumph together as young lions. As brothers. He fights to be the one to bring home the kill to our mother. I know he just wants a chance for her to see him—he never played with her through the roses, never felt her paws collapsing his chest. I fight him back but let him win every time. I already know what it's like to be seen.

The ways of man take up most of our days. I show him all of the things to keep his body well, how to cover its weakness in clothing to stay warm, how to feed it with things no lion would ever touch, and I bring him to school where he resists, "Let's go home. Let's be lions!" I shush him and explain, "Learn all the things they teach you so you can be free to be a lion. Like mother did, like father did." The mention of "father" always quiets him. It's a tool that hurts but I use it often because it's hard raising a cub that isn't yours. It's hard being everything for everyone when you just want to be someone else's everything.

At night we go to sleep as lions. Lions, but still cubs.

We join our mother in her part of the den. She is so massive. She is the biggest thing in our lives.

We curl up next to her warmth which is all she has left to give.

~ 23.
Today I Am A Meat Cutter

Today I am a meat cutter. There is so much meat in the world, and every day I am so sad to be cutting it.

"Woe is me!" I cry, so buried with the weight of my professional burden. The weight of slaughtered gore.

It is so damned heavy.

It crushes.

I blame my father. A meat cutter himself. He put on the parental pressure, "Son, if you don't grow up to cut meat for a living, God be with you." Huffing it in a manner that meant exactly what I thought it meant— "Fuck you if you don't cut meat."

After the divorce, my mom became a vegetarian. He forbade us to speak her name.

Her name is Helen.

I come home every night smelling of death. My wife can't get the smell of blood out of my clothes. But she likes it. Always wanting me to fuck her while still wearing my bloody apron. My hair net. My elastic paper booties. She rubs her face in the mess. When I kiss her; bits of bone, fat.

She is a meal I made her become.

One bad cut can fuck up a steak. I've only made two bad cuts my entire life. One got me fired, the other I cried over.

Hate fucking up a good primal cut. Like throwing money into a campfire.

Money that used to breathe and eat grass.

See all of my knives? All of them so sharp they can cut breath. My little soldiers. My good friends.

On my dark days, it's not cows I am cutting.

~ 24.
Today I Am A Mess

Today I am a mess. You are gone and I am made of wood. The sap in my veins runs hard. I have become a fence post, a "KEEP OUT" sign, a tree-swing seat, rope-threaded. Where did my soft go? Did you take it with you? Predictable. As always, you stealing my soft.

Remember back when? All your whites, white? It's hard now, with everything so long yellowed. I still have pictures. There's still proof.

Earlier, when the bell rang, God said, "Are you happy now" telling me, not asking. It was then I knew. I had been waiting a month for that bell.

I did not answer God. He knows the guilt in my belly.

Last night when I cried into your neck while you slept, quiet-sobbing those words into the fold of your ear, I hope you heard me. I hope you understood. If the guarantee of your understanding those words could be traded for all previous—all words before turned to nonsense—I would beg God to have made it so.

All meaning in lifetime words pale in the light of the meaning of those spoken last.

There is a hole back home waiting for me to step into it. And while I know it will break my legs, I am so thankful you were there to dig it.

~ 25.
Today I Am A Hypnotist

Today I am a hypnotist. I do not want to force you, but as I've said, the sensible thing is "sustaining." Making and keeping everything in the place it is supposed to be. You are here now. In this place. With me. You staying here will result in forward movement. If you leave now, you will only move backward. I am asking you, with the plainest of words, to please stay. Sustain. It's for your own good.

"I will stay."

Good. Now, please do as you've done before. Give me the minutes to take you there. I will start with the motion and then the sound. When the sinking begins, discard all fear. The place is waiting for you. It wants you. Do you feel it?

"Yes."

Good.

Now relax.

Now breathe.

....
....
....
....
....
...
..
.

Have you arrived?

"Yes."

How long have you been there?

"1,949 years."

How long can you stay?

"Only minutes."

Then tell me. As much as you can, as fast as you can.
When you feel the pull begin, let it take you and I will
catch you upon entry.

Go.

"They were webbed. All of them. Again, crawling and vicious. And when I climbed through and got behind them, I found the room. It smelled as it had smelled before and I winced. I did not want to go in! (*crying*) I called out to you, 'Do not make me go in!' but you did not answer and I thought, "sustain." (*crying*) And I went. The air inside was stagnant-warm and palpable. I wanted to wipe it from my skin but it was nothing. The light was ample but I could only bring myself to see the walls, the floor, the curtains, the ceiling but not the bed. (*crying*) I took small steps forward avoiding him until I could no longer. His breathing found me first. A straw-like husk sound and it froze me. I forced my eyes to find him and there he was. A feminine thing now. No trace of masculinity; his countenance paste and wisp, his hair blinding white and frothed. He was asleep and so I stared. His mouth pulled open and back. His teeth long, gums gray and receded. His face, skeletal. I wanted to run but then your voice came, ordering, 'Sustain!' and so I did! (*crying*) I walked forward to touch him, even though it was furthest from anything I wanted to do but I felt it what was needed. I searched his hand with my eyes, making sure there were no webs and then I reached for it. My hand seemed so massive above his which was this shrunken thing and suddenly I felt no fear, only sadness. But then he grabbed me and I leapt! His strength was nothing that I've ever felt before! It was as if his hand was a steel trap! I couldn't move! He had me! I couldn't move! (*shrieking*) (*crying*) He pulled me toward him. Slow, but strong, and I could do nothing! (*stammering*) (*moaning*) Oh, yes! The pull! Oh, blessed pull! (*sobbing*)"

Let it take you. I will be here when you return. You did well.

Very well.

~ 26.
Today I Am A Missing
Ten Year Old

Today I am a missing ten year old. There are 33 of us. When I got here there were 17. The crying was bad then, now it's horrible. I know it will settle down in a few days. The ones that have been here the longest no longer cry. They are little roly-poly balls that stink, all gray and rocking. The newest ones wail loudest, still fresh on Cheerios, Capri Sun and Cartoon Network. They haven't stared out of these bars for hours, haven't been dulled by all of the nothing. Give them time.

The cage is big and very tall. There are bunk beds. My bunk is one second from the bottom. If I lean over and look up, I can barely see the topmost bunks. There are lots of skinny ladders whose tops disappear into a wall of flapping sheets, swinging legs and stretching arms. It looks like the outsides of skyscrapers people are try-ing to escape from. Things keep falling, both dry and wet. It's a different type of weather in here and there's no way to get away from it.

A while ago they gave us a Doberman Pinscher puppy named Rita. It was dressed in doll clothes. It got passed around. It was fought over like a new toy. There was the crying and there was the screaming over who gets Rita next, and then there was the sound when four kids got Rita at the same time.

That day had the worst weather.

Some kids get taken out, but they are few. At first I thought they were taking only the good kids, or the ones that stopped making noise or moving. But they take any kind of kid: the boy that kept jumping off the ladders, the girl with the screaming nightmares, the girl who kept stealing all the pillows, the boy who kept banging his head into the bars, the boy who played with all the poo. All of them taken and gone. Their beds are now filled by new kids.

New kids keep coming and coming. Nothing is clean anymore. It i's never quiet. I can't get warm. I am always hungry. Even when I'm sleeping. I can't stop rocking now. My hands around my knees. Back and forth, back and forth. And even though it scares me I can't stop. It's the only thing that feels good.

Everyone wants their mother. Not me. I want my dad. I want us to play airplanes. I want his tickles and story-times. I want his big hands to pull me out of this cage. Pull me out like I am a hamster. I want him to carry me on his shoulders to his truck. I want him to ask me if I'm all belted in, boy. When I am bad, he has a way where he shakes me. It's like he's using all of his muscles to knock the bad in me loose. Like he's a bunch of scared ten year olds and I am a puppy dressed in doll clothes. I don't even care about that anymore. I just want to be found.

~ 27.
Today I Am A King

Today I am a king. Remember when *you* were a king? How we bowed down before you? The way you wore your crown? Down low, where everyone could touch it if they wanted to?

And they all wanted to.

We all wanted to.

I wanted to.

Your height prevented our hording. The massive mountain of you like Barthelme's "Dead Father." How you towered. Unreachable. The thunder of your steps on the stone.

So many nights dreaming of becoming a limb on the tree of you. My fingers busy making the dream as real as I could. My body a branch of five; two behind you and three in front. Your trunk the rhythmic wind, bouncing me above the forest. Our bodies coming together in a beautiful fork, the sweat of our leaves.

Oh my King! Yes, my king!!

The darkness of your chamber, illuminated in a white glow, capped by red from a source unseen. Your massive throne that propped the straight of your spine. Oh, how regal you were! My visits just to be in your presence. To curtsy, and bow low enough to let you see what I wanted you to. To sit on the ground before you, your subject.

Oh, when you were king!

But now, I am king.

~ 28.
Today I Am A Parking Lot Guy

Today I am a parking lot guy. I am standing just beyond the cement, right where the asphalt begins to surge. I trade surfaces for hours: gray, black, gray, black, gray, black. My sign says it all: *PARKING*: $15. Like that's all you need to know. Like that's all you think I have to tell you.

Sometimes I sing. The songs are varied but important. If anyone stopped to listen...all these cars with their windows rolled up, rolled down, mid-way....they would hear their lives sung back to them. They'd know why they were here. They'd know their purpose.

But nobody does.

They just see 'old black guy, parking lot guy, no teeth guy, sign swaying, $15 guy." They don't see "soothsayer. "

The cars swing past me. Some so close I feel their heat, the thrum of their motor. I want to slap them. I want to make them see more than my sign.

I sing all of their songs. Songs specifically FOR them. And all I hear is Bruno Mars and Pitbull. All I hear are songs that are what they think music should be.

My sign sometimes says PARKING: $20. Sometimes, *PARKING*: $10. Whatever it says, it's always in the same black Sharpie. Whatever it says, I'm always stepping between the gray and black, singing the songs they wished they'd heard me sing.

~ 29.
Today I Am A Burglar

Today I am a burglar. With all it entails. Things like, danger, high-speed chases, ketamine, Rachel Ray on the Tivo and tennis club memberships. I even have a secret crawl space for when the going gets tough. There is a lot of tough going in the burglary game. I call it a game sometimes because I base my life on a series of points. Currently I am at 7,450,980,033 points. Last week I was at 7,450,979,452 but then I killed this one guy (his fault) and I accidentally procured 40 crates of fresh Florida grapefruit. Grapefruits? Whichever way, they now belong to me and now I have more points than I did before.

I have a lot of points.

Currently, my mom thinks I am a freelancer. At what? I don't know. I keep things very vague with her. Sometimes I say circusy shit or mountain climbing shit or symphony orchestra cello shit. Once she called me while I was stuck on top of this chain link pen full of pit bulls and told her I was really busy with work and I started panting and grunting and shit and I think that confused her face off. I think about what she must tell her friends about me and I laugh my fucking ass off.

My favorite part of burglaring is the clothing. There is a lot of good active wear out there on the market now. A lot of breathable material, yoga-flexible. Curves nicely against my muscular ass. (670 points currently) The face paint is dope. I have big knives and leather straps all over the place. Ninja-ish. Wigs are so many extra points, especially any blonde ones longer than shoulder length I'm a dude.

Sometimes I sport a colorful scarf. (48 points)

I have 14 storage facilities. One of them has a live owl. (4,329 points)

Today I am a burglar and tomorrow I might pull a heist. Or I might just break in somewhere and steal shit.

Steal shit = take shit that ain't mine.

I have a chest of gold doubloons. Not lying. Stole it from an actual pirate. (9,659 points)

The best thing I ever burgled was your mom.

And she fucking loved it.

(infinity points)

~ 30.
Today I Am A Make Up Artist

Today I am a make up artist. Every day, really. It makes life more interesting. Better.

It started when I was young. There was a period of six years when I lived every day as a boy. Cut my hair short, wore my brother's clothes, peed standing up, chased and pinched the girls, played tackle football, went fishing with my uncle, wiped snots on the wall by my bed, stole my dad's Playboys. I made everyone call me Lee Van (my given name being, "Leigh Ann"). My mom tells me now that if she hadn't have spent 2-5 of my primordial years cleaning my vagina she would've thought I had a penis. My dad started to scruff my hair, called me, "son." Finally let me bring him his beer, change the channels for him, get him the newspaper. Made my brother jealous until I hit puberty and my dad took me back off the roster. He couldn't call me "son" with my new titties poking up my shirts.

But my breasts coming in didn't stop me. I still made stuff up. I'd mess around and stuff my bra big as a house one day, duck egg the next. I've had more wigs and hair colors then a beauty salon. Fake nails, ass-plumping pads, hair extensions. It's easy to be a make-up artist when you're a female. So much of what we're meant to be is pretend, anyway.

Nowadays I can't go as big as before, when I was young. Today I have to be more accountable. Instead I have to resort to little things like giving the guy at Starbucks a fake name just so I can see it black Sharpied on the cup, putting the wrong weight on my driver's license, telling a handful of soccer moms I used to be a phone sex operator, managing a couple of young men online who both think I'm their girlfriend, microwave dinner then put it on plates like it was from scratch and not out of a box or plastic bag, convincing my boss I am completely on top of things, assuring my two kids that everything will be okay, telling my husband I love him.

Every day can be a fun day when you are a make up artist.

~ 31.
Today I Am A Writer

Today I am a writer. I say this thirty-three times while forcefully bashing my head into the metal keys of a typewriter. I want the letters to imprint my face. I want its ribbon to birth answers. Tell me what I need to say. Instead, the type bars jam together: f, g, j, m and b. Their skinny heads all vying for first place. All the blood mars any facial embossing and I am still sitting where I began—blank.

I wear dark-rimmed glasses and knitted scarves. Still nothing. I try a beard and skinny jeans. It starts to feel hopeful so I use a small handcart to push my typewriter to Starbucks. I sit in the back, around the corner from the barista. I put two tables together and ask a larger man than myself to lift the typewriter to the table top. I watch his forehead pop a vein. He tells me, "Nice scarf." I thank him and settle in.

The paper stays blank through "Peppermint Mocha for Jeff" and "Vanilla Chai for Dave." By the time Christy, Rebecca and Steve get their drinks my raised hands are cramping. Their poise above the keys threatening like crows ready to dive. I can't take them away. If I do, the keys will know they've won. Under this aggressive stance they cower dully. Inside I am pulling everything

I can so I can ruin that white sheet of paper. Deface its empty with lines of black. But nothing comes forward. I can almost hear the paper laughing.

Troy gets a non-fat mocha, Stacy gets an upside-down caramel Macchiato, Terrell, a Frappuccino and I am doing all I can to not smash my face back into the keys again. But I can't. Not now. Not while they are scared.

There is an arctic buzzing noise that builds around me in a hummingbird heartbeat sort of way. It grows hard and spines through my skull and into my brain. Right as it's beginning to nest, right as I am fearing its constricted, twisting ball and the babies it will birth, I am ripped out of it. Its strands fall behind me where I've been sitting, coiling and uncoiling wildly against the warmth I've left there.

"Get the fuck out of here!" the guy says. He's holding me at my shoulders, compressing them with an intense pulse. I am an accordion then I am on the sidewalk. Then my typewriter. Then my hand cart. All of us thrust out and landing on the cement like clowns. I want to load us both onto the hand cart and somehow push ourselves back to my apartment. But I am not three people. I am only one.

I first see the blood on the sidewalk. I don't see it on my face until I stand up and turn towards all the people staring at me through the window of Starbucks.

In my reflection, the blood looks black. It's a straight line across my forehead and then stretched tines down the length of my face. They are thick and meaningful. More than anything I've yet to put on the page. I gather my things and go.

Later, when I wash the blood off my face, I see the letters. It's all backwards in the mirror but I love it. Only two lines, but they churn the stagnant inside me. I towel off and begin to repair my typewriter before it has a chance to fade.

~ 32.
Today I Am A Nun

Today I am a nun. Yellow and blue make green. Water is the absence of color. Drop a red marker into the water, watch the liquid draw its stain. Take a Bic lighter to a brown crayon. Melt it all over your boyfriend's white back. Tell him you are turning him negro. Ask how he likes that. Now...and here is the important part...make him a cheese omelet. Put the plate out in front of him. No fork. Start peeling the dried brown spots from his back while he does his best to scoop-eat the omelet into his mouth. Now, while he's vulnerable, talk about your vows.

Your vows are like colors, you say. Egg yolk-yellow is how you'll never again masturbate in the bath. The prayers you whisper are all cornflower blue. The men who will never again enter you are darkening shades of orange. Vermilion is the color of every dirty word you now swallow instead of speak.

"Punch my guts," you dare him. "Watch how they'll spill out red and chunky."

Make the next omelet cheese-side out. Slap it on his back. As the cheese burns, take his screams from his mouth with your own. Leave his tongue sitting in his mouth, meadow green.

Dress every day in all black and hardly white. Stand in the kaleidoscope patches made from the sun shining through the stained glass. Stand so that the colors paint your face. Your face full of vows.

~ 33.
Today I Am A Horse Whisperer

Today I am a horse whisperer. My throat is clogged with phlegm. The morning coughing is the worst, but I like it. The gooey shit. The gunk that comes warm-splat into my mouth and makes itself known, demands acknowledgement, like Kramer entering Seinfeld's apartment.

I spit it into the belly of my palm, poke it around with my finger. Slide it into the sink.

But this cough. It doesn't want to leave me. It lingers. The horses shy from me now. I startle them. The hack, gunshots. What smart animal doesn't run from gun-shots? And horses are *very* smart. Trust me. I know.

It's affecting my work. All day they scatter from me like pigeons from terrorist children. I try pulling them back with the whispers, but it's damn near impossible. They're fucking far away and I'm fucking whispering. The physics of it make it a completely useless endeav-or. I should just go home. Wish I was a horse shouter sometimes. They have those, you know. It's what us whisperers derived from. You can't keep all that shout-ing up without fucking up your throat. There aren't many of them left now. They should've seen it coming.

Let's be honest.

The horses have a punishing darkness. It's why I got into this. I live to take it away. I live to make them lighter.

When I receive from the horses it feels like an electrical charge. There's a heat to it, but it's a spicy one. Like the flame you get in your mouth after chewing a toxic pepper, but unrelenting and hard and jabbing through your skin.

They send it to me in a way that I call, "The Bore." It drills in through different places: my shoulders, my spine, calve, wrist, knee. It comes in, rounds through, and lets itself out, inside of me. Only after its done all this do I receive.

I wonder if they take my whispers in the same way.

No matter. It's a giving and a taking and both again and always.

I wonder if they ever want to run their brawn against barb wire fences until their skin splits.

No I don't.

I already know.

If this cough persists for one more day, there will be problems. I can already see the thunder-twitch in their hind quarters. I see their eyes hunting for the sharp of broken wood.

I'm going to get some hot tea and I'm going to sip it until it melts through the mucus. I'm going to keep trying to get close to them. I'm not going to give up. I can't. I must try. It's my duty.

~ 34.
Today I Am A Flower Girl

Today I am a flower girl. Look at my dress! Look how its frill presses against me like death! My father's hands now satin and lace. My father's hands all at once. My father's hands all over and brazen. The colored shine through the stained glass windows tainting the white like it knows.

I knew the church would know.

The shadow of its steeples caught and caressed me when I approached. I stepped left and right but no matter. I was a fly. I was a small mouse.

Such insignificant things cannot run so easy from darkness.

Such insignificant things cannot hide their darkness so easily.

Today I am a flower girl. See the basket that waits for me! Overflowing with petals I am meant to scatter. I have practiced for days. Grabbing air, lifting air, dropping air. My gaze straight ahead and even. My gaze on an imaginary place, far far away.

Grabbing air,

lifting air,

dropping air.

Look at my dress! Watch how I twirl! See how it becomes a radius around me! As if it thinks I am the sun! As if it wants to show the world that I am the vital part of a blossom!

I love this dress. Truly, I do.

~ 35.
Today I Am A Summer Field

Today I am a summer field. Put yourself inside me. Watch what I do when the wind blows. Thread through the stems that stream me. Feel my skin from the sun. Put your face against mine. Let them melt-stick together. Let them become one giant face. A four-eyed, two-mouthed, mass of wrong. An outside reflecting my in but at least that means we're forever together.

In the summer field of me we can entwine; our freak-face head atop our bodies now forced to know one another as their own. The warm dirt dusting our forms in blessing.

The field spreads wide, singing of childhood. That's why it is me. That's why I want you there. You are the hand dropped down for me to hold. To hold on to.

Oh, to be lifted apart from this field!

When we are together in the summer field, you will be bigger than me. It's your duty. It's my prayer. For once, a blockade comes for me. Your mass of stone surrounding me as arms of a protective father might.

Should.

There are those that don't. There are father's arms that carry you through the corn, so much corn, that for a while you think the flapping of their leaves against your feet and face is a mass of green birds angry with your intrusion. When the corn finally ends and the birds abate there is the peace of a summer field. Its grasses as high as the corn. Its still settles on you like baby's breath.

The father's arms set you down because the father's mouth tells you about the secrets you will find in this field. Together. You don't know anything yet so you ask him where they are and he says, "We need to walk until we can't see the corn anymore. That's where we will find them."

It's a short walk, but you find the secrets. A treasure trove. And when you are carried back through the corn the birds' wings are nothing at all and your father is humming a melody you will never be able to forget.

But in *this* summer field I have you. And your arms have only carried me *out* of the corn. And your mouth has never told promises of finding secrets. And when they command, "Show me on the doll where he touched you," *you* will take that doll, *you* will touch that doll everywhere he did not. With that action, forecasting a new weather.

You will hand me the doll, a gift. The chaste and un-spoiled doll. We will bury it in me. The soil will accept it and my field will sing a different childhood song. A song of a new summer field, one that does not shelter what happens beneath its tall grasses, one that does not have mixed liquids soaked into its soil, one that releases instead of takes. And one day, because of you, the father's melody will finally be forgotten; in its place, this new song.

OFFICIAL

CCM ◗

GET OUT OF JAIL
* VOUCHER *

- -

Tear this out.
Skip that social event.
It's okay.
You don't have to go if you don't want to. Pick up
the book you just bought. Open to the first page.
You'll thank us by the third paragraph.

If friends ask why you were a no-show, show them
this voucher.
You'll be fine.

- -

We're coping.

◗

CPSIA information can be obtained
at www.ICGtesting.com
Printed in the USA
BVOW03s1601260117
474419BV00003B/229/P